DREAMWORKS

KUNG·FU
PANDA
2

The Novel

D0169927

The Novel

by Tracey West

PSS!
PRICE STERN SLOAN

An Imprint of Penguin Group (USA) Inc.

PRICE STERN SLOAN
Published by the Penguin Group
Penguin Group (USA) Inc., 375 Hudson Street, New York,
New York 10014, USA
Penguin Group (Canada), 90 Eglinton Avenue East, Suite 700,
Toronto, Ontario M4P 2Y3, Canada
(a division of Pearson Penguin Canada Inc.)
Penguin Books Ltd., 80 Strand, London WC2R 0RL, England
Penguin Group Ireland, 25 St. Stephen's Green, Dublin 2, Ireland
(a division of Penguin Books Ltd.)
Penguin Group (Australia), 250 Camberwell Road, Camberwell, Victoria 3124,
Australia (a division of Pearson Australia Group Pty. Ltd.)
Penguin Books India Pvt. Ltd., 11 Community Centre, Panchsheel Park,
New Delhi—110 017, India
Penguin Group (NZ), 67 Apollo Drive, Rosedale, North Shore 0632, New
Zealand (a division of Pearson New Zealand Ltd.)
Penguin Books (South Africa) (Pty.) Ltd., 24 Sturdee Avenue,
Rosebank, Johannesburg 2196, South Africa

Penguin Books Ltd., Registered Offices: 80 Strand,
London WC2R 0RL, England

Kung Fu Panda 2 ™ & © 2011 DreamWorks Animation L.L.C. Kung Fu Panda
® DreamWorks Animation L.L.C. Published by Price Stern Sloan,
a division of Penguin Young Readers Group, 345 Hudson Street, New York,
New York, 10014. PSS! is a registered trademark of Penguin Group (USA) Inc.
Printed in the U.S.A.

ISBN 978-0-8431-9859-1   10 9 8 7 6 5 4 3 2 1

PROLOGUE

Long ago, the peacocks of Gongmen City created a thing of great beauty: fireworks. For generations the fireworks brought joy to the city. But one young peacock wondered if the flames held even greater power.

Shen was a peacock with feathers as white as the winter snow. He spent hours in the darkness of his room experimenting with the black powder that created the dazzling light shows in the sky. But Shen wasn't making fireworks. Instead he imagined great weapons capable of deadly force.

Lord and Lady Peacock turned to wise Soothsayer. An old goat, Soothsayer mixed herbs and oils until a cloud of smoke shot up, forming the black and white symbol of yin and yang. Soothsayer warned that if Shen continued down the path he was on, he would be stopped by a warrior of black and white.

Young Shen tried to change his fate, but what he did next only sealed it. He gathered a small army of wolf guards and attacked a village of peaceful panda farmers.

His parents were horrified by what their son had done. They banished him from the city. As he stormed away from the Palace, Shen swore he would return and bring his fiery vengeance upon all of China.

Years later, Shen was ready to keep his promise. Clouds of hot steam puffed, hissed, and billowed inside an old fireworks factory. Sparks flew as workers shaped the red-hot metal with their hammers.

One of the wolf leaders kneeled before his master, a cloaked figure with metal claws.

"It's almost done, Lord Shen," the wolf leader reported. "But we need more metal."

Shen nodded. "Go to the farthest village and get the metal," he replied. "Then we get the black powder. Then . . . we get the world."

CHAPTER 1

Forty Bean Buns

The sun dawned gently that morning in the Valley of Peace. The bright rays shone through the windows of the Furious Five's training barracks. Viper, Crane, Mantis, Tigress, and Monkey were gathered around the Dragon Warrior.

"Thirty-four!" yelled the Five. "Stop him! It's too dangerous! Thirty-five! Thirty-six! Thirty-seven!"

"How is he doing that with his face?" asked Mantis.

The Five stopped and studied Po, the Dragon Warrior, a large panda with a round belly. He was stuffing dumplings into his mouth with a pair of chopsticks. His furry cheeks looked like they couldn't fit another bite.

But Po shoved one last dumpling into his mouth, and then pounded his fist on the table in front of him.

"Thirty-eight bean buns!" he cried triumphantly through a mouth full of food.

"Ahh! It's too horrible," Viper cried.

But Mantis cheered. "Yeah! New record! You monster!" The little green insect waved his front legs.

"More! Hit forty!" Monkey urged.

Po's face turned red. He started to mumble something, but he couldn't form the words.

"Are you choking?" Crane asked.

Po tried to answer but he couldn't. His mouth was too full.

"Do you need me to hit you on the back?" Crane asked.

Po mumbled something else.

"Is that a *yes*?" Crane asked.

Po quickly stuffed two more dumplings

in his mouth.

"Thirty-nine, forty!" he cried triumphantly. Then he dashed out—he was late for training with Master Shifu.

CHAPTER 2

"Inner Peace! Inner Peace!"

Today Master Shifu was teaching Po in the Dragon Grotto, a mountain cave set above a waterfall. Inside the cave, a dragon statue stood over a lake of deep blue water. Water dripped down from the ceiling. *Plunk, plunk, plunk.*

Master Shifu was balancing on one leg on top of his staff, which stood straight up in the middle of the lake. One twitch and he would plunge into the cold water below.

"Inner Peace. Inner Peace," he repeated calmly.

Then he heard Po huffing and puffing his way up the mountain. His inner calm began to waver.

"Inner Peace," he said, trying not to wobble.

Po came rushing into the cave, splashing through the water.

"Master Shifu! Master Shifu!" he cried. Then he stopped, surprised to see his teacher balanced on top of the tall staff. "Uh, what—"

"*Shh!*"

"Are—" Po didn't get it.

"*Shh!*"

"You—" Po still didn't get it.

"*Shh!*"

Po finally caught on, but he still couldn't help himself. "Doing?" he asked in a whisper.

A drop of water fell from the cave ceiling. Shifu closed his eyes in concentration. He gracefully slid his right arm in front of his body, catching the water droplet gently in his hand. Then he turned over his palm, and the unbroken drop fell onto a small plant sprouting through the stone floor.

"Awesome!" Po cried. "How. Did. You.

DO THAT?"

"Inner Peace," Shifu replied.

"That's cool," Po said. He paused. "I have no idea what that means."

"It is the next phase of your training," Shifu replied. "Every master must find his path to Inner Peace. Some choose to meditate for fifty years. In a cave, just like this. Without the slightest taste of food or water."

Po's stomach growled just thinking about it. There had to be another way.

"Or . . . ?" Po asked.

"Some find it through pain and suffering," Shifu answered. "As I did. Po, the day you were chosen as the Dragon Warrior . . . was the worst day of my life."

Po gave a sheepish shrug.

"By far, nothing else comes close," Shifu continued. "It was the worst, most unbearable, saddest—"

"Okay," Po interrupted. He had heard enough. But Shifu wasn't finished.

"—most painful, mind-destroyingly horrible

moment I have ever experienced," he finished with a shudder. "But once I realized the problem was not you, but within me, I found Inner Peace and was able to harness the flow of the universe."

"So that's it? I just need some peace?" Po asked. He patted his tummy. "I'm pretty peaceful in my innards. All right, let's do it. Inner Peace, you're going down! All right! It's on! Show me that water drop thingy. What *was* that?"

Po mimicked Shifu's movements, sliding his arms in front of himself as a drop of water fell from the ceiling . . .

"Po!"

Po looked up to see Tigress in the mouth of the cave.

"Bandits! Approaching the Musician's Village!" she called out. Po could hear a warning bell chiming in the distance.

"Danger!" Po cried. "Tell those musicians to start playing some action music because it is ON!"

9

He ran out of the cave.

"No snack stops this time," Tigress told him.

"Forty bean buns! You think I still need to eat?" Po shot back. "I mean, I could, but I won't."

The two warriors hurried off to save the village.

CHAPTER 3

"My Fist Hungers for Justice!"

The alarm came from a small village nestled in the hills. The artisans who lived there made their living crafting musical instruments. Some made flutes from bamboo that sounded like singing birds. Others carved percussion instruments from wood or hammered metal into loud gongs or delicate wind chimes. But this morning, the only instrument being played was a massive warning bell.

Clang! Clang! Clang! A nervous bunny sounded the alarm as wolf bandits dropped down from the sky on ropes attached to grappling hooks. The wolves tore through the village, scrambling across rooftops and crashing through doors and windows.

"Get all of the metal you can find!" the wolf leader ordered.

The bandits obeyed, ransacking each hut and grabbing every metal chime, gong, bell, and cymbal they could.

"Get those metal drums!" one of the bandits yelled.

The villagers screamed and ran.

"Help! Help! Help! Help! Help!" cried a pudgy pig apprentice. He ducked under a giant bell. But a group of wolves found the bell and rolled it away—with the pig trapped inside. They joined the rest of the bandits, who were tying the loot in bundles and attaching them to the ropes.

"That's everything. Let's get out of here!" barked the wolf leader.

"Oh no!" the pig wailed from inside the bell.

Then a powerful cry rang across the mountainside.

"Waahooooooo!"

The bandits turned to see six figures on a cliff just above the village. Viper slithered across the rocks. Tigress bounded alongside her. Monkey, with golden fur, kept pace as Mantis balanced on his shoulder. Crane flew overhead. Leading them all was a large, round panda.

"Wings of Justice!" yelled Po.

Po leaped off of the cliff and plummeted down the mountainside with a rousing cry.

"Yahoooooooooooo!"

Crane swooped in and hurled Po forward. The panda and the other warriors landed right in the center of the village. Each one struck a battle pose, ready to fight. It would have been a really impressive scene—except that Po was facing backward.

"Huh?" Po realized his mistake and turned around. "Ha ha!"

"The Dragon Warrior!" cried a rabbit in the crowd. The villagers let out a cheer.

The wolf leader growled. "A panda? Impossible!"

13

"My fist hungers for justice!" Po yelled. Then his bouncy stomach let out a loud growl. "Uh, that was my fist."

The wolf leader pointed to his bandits. "Get him!"

"Come on," Po said eagerly.

The bandits charged forward, and Po and the Furious Five bravely faced them.

Mantis used his amazing strength to push a blind rabbit playing a harp to safety. Monkey grabbed two long flutes and used them as fighting staffs to keep the wolves at bay. Tigress tossed wolves over her shoulder like they were rag dolls.

A wolf brandishing a heavy mace swung it at Viper. She wrapped her tail around the weapon's long handle and sent the bandit flying into a large drum. He bounced off of it and landed on his back with a thud.

"Take that!" Viper cried.

Po pounded on two attacking wolves with a large drum mallet. Then the wolf leader sent more bandits into the fray. Three bandits raced toward Po, shooting arrows at him.

"Po! Incoming!" Mantis warned.

Mantis reached for a crate of small cymbals and sent them flying through the air.

Clang! Clang! Clang! Clang! The cymbals blocked each one of the arrows.

"Thanks, Mantis!" Po called out.

Then two sword-wielding bandits ran at Po. He lifted up a large harp to block the blows. The metal swords made a horrible screeching sound as they hit the strings.

Another group of wolves flung sharp axes at Po. He ran as fast as he could and took cover behind a hut. The axes thudded into the hut's wooden wall. Po gripped the ax handles and used them to climb to the roof. The wolves followed behind, grabbing onto Po's ankles.

"Tigress! Double Death Strike!" Po yelled.

Tigress leaped onto the roof and grabbed Po. She whirled him around, sending the wolves flying. Then she flung Po into the air like a missile, aiming him at another group of wolves jumping onto the roof.

"Feet of Fury!" Po cried.

He kicked the wolves and they crashed to the ground below. Then, before Po could fall, Crane swooped in and deposited Po safely on the ground.

The Furious Five gathered around Po. He picked up his teammates one by one and flung them at the charging bandits.

"Tigress! Monkey! Viper! Mantis! Bunny! What?"

Po realized he had accidentally picked up the blind rabbit, who was oblivious to the chaos around him.

"Oh, sorry," Po said.

The remaining wolves ran back to their leader, who gave a loud howl. The noise signaled a massive gorilla waiting in the mists above. With a mighty heave, the gorilla pulled up the ropes tied to the bags of stolen instruments. Inside the big bell, the terrified apprentice pig let out a scream.

"Ah! Help!"

"Crane, go!" Po ordered.

"I'm on it," Crane replied. He soared upward, slicing through the ropes with his beak. The bell—with the pig inside it—cascaded toward a deep gorge.

"Whoa!" Po cried in alarm. He leaped to catch the falling bell. Viper latched onto him with her tail, and Monkey grabbed onto Viper. Tigress caught Monkey's tail, keeping them all from falling into the abyss.

With a hard yank, Tigress pulled everyone to safety on solid ground. The bell bounced toward Mantis, who grunted as he stopped it from rolling away. The apprentice pig stepped out, a little dizzy, but safe at last.

"Is everyone okay?" Po asked.

The crowd let out a cheer. Crane had sliced through rope after rope, sending the stolen loot dropping into the gorge—and out of the hands of the bandits. The wolf leader's face turned dark as he watched his prizes disappear. He raised a large battle hammer and charged right at Po.

"I got this," Po said confidently.

The wolf leader raised the hammer to strike. That's when Po noticed the symbol on the wolf's uniform—a large eye.

Po gasped and then froze. A terrifying vision washed over him . . . a glowing red eye . . . a tiny panda baby crying . . . a panda mother.

"Po!" Tigress shouted.

But her warning came too late. The hammer smacked into Po, sending him flying. He collided with Tigress and several of the bunny villagers. The wolf leader jumped on top of the last bag of loot, and the gorilla pulled him up and away into the mountain mists.

The squashed bunnies groaned under Po's big belly.

"Help!" squeaked the blind bunny.

With a grunt, Mantis heaved Po to his feet, and the rabbits rolled to safety. The Five gathered around him, concerned.

Viper looked worried. "Oh, sweetie, are

you okay?"

"What happened?" asked Tigress.

Po still felt like he was in a daze. The vision had been real . . . *too* real. But where had it come from?

"I . . . I don't know."

CHAPTER 4

"Xiao Po, My Little Panda"

The strange vision still haunted Po after they had left the small village. He went to visit the only one who might be able to help him figure it out—his father.

When Po reached his dad's noodle shop, Mr. Ping was busily moving between the tables on the crowded patio. A white goose with a long neck, Mr. Ping wore a red silk jacket. He carried a porcelain teapot in his right wing and a tray of white soup bowls in the other. He waved to a satisfied duck and rabbit who put down their coins and walked away from their table.

"Thank you for coming to Dragon Warrior

Noodles and Tofu," he called out happily. He turned to the table next to him. "More tea? Lemon sauce? If you need anything, just ask. Thank you!"

Not long ago, the shop had been a simple noodle shop. But ever since his son, Po, had become the Dragon Warrior, Mr. Ping's business was booming.

Two young bunnies wrestled between the tables, making kung fu moves.

"Feet of Fury!" a little brown rabbit cried, kicking his furry foot.

Two more rabbits stared at a mop mounted on the wall.

"The Dragon Warrior's mop!" the bunny gasped. "He mopped these very floors!"

He reached out to touch the mop, but Mr. Ping scolded him. "No touching! You'll get the mop dirty."

At another table, two plump pigs were talking about the Dragon Warrior.

"He once waited on me!" bragged the first pig.

"Awesome!" said his friend.

"Yeah, I have the stain to prove it," the pig said, looking down at his shirt. He nodded to Mr. Ping. "Hey, where's the Dragon Warrior?"

"Oh, he doesn't work here anymore," the goose replied with a wave of his wing. "He's busy out there. Protecting the Valley."

Then the pig let out a cry of surprise and pointed. "The Dragon Warrior!"

Customers crowded around Po as he stepped onto the patio. Po wasn't sure how to react. Not long ago, he had been a simple busboy in a noodle shop. He was still getting used to being a hero.

Mr. Ping rushed over to Po and gave him a hug. "You should have told me you were coming. I would have saved you some stinky tofu."

Po took the tray of bowls from his dad. "Uh, Dad. Can I talk to you?"

"Of course, son," Mr. Ping replied. He turned to the crowd. "In honor of my son, free tofu dessert for everybody!"

"Yaaaay!" the crowd cheered.

"With purchases!" Mr. Ping added.

The crowd whined. "Awww . . ."

Po followed his dad into the kitchen where steaming pots of noodle soup bubbled away.

"It's so good to see you, Po," Mr. Ping chattered. "Have you lost weight? I can almost put my wings around you."

"Ah, well, maybe a little," Po replied.

"Oh, poor you! You must feel weak! Let me get you some soup."

Mr. Ping picked up his cleaver and began chopping vegetables at the counter. He never liked to stay still for long.

"Ah, no, that's okay, Dad. I'm not hungry," Po told him.

Mr. Ping frowned. "Not hungry? Po, are you all right?"

"Yeah, yeah, I'm fine," Po said quickly. "It's just . . . earlier today I was fighting these bandits. Nothing too dangerous. And then the strangest thing happened. Uh, I had this crazy vision. I think I saw my mom. And me . . . as a baby?"

Mr. Ping stopped chopping for a moment. Then his cleaver moved again, chopping faster than ever before.

"Huh? What? Mom? A baby?"

Po stared at the picture of himself and his dad on the counter. Mr. Ping, a small goose, with his arm around Po, a large panda. Po loved his dad so much. But it was time for the truth to come out.

"Um, Dad, how do I say this?" Po found his courage. "Where did I come from?"

Po's father stopped chopping and turned to face his son.

"Well, you see, son, baby geese come from a little egg," Mr. Ping began. "Don't ask me where the egg comes from."

"Dad, that's not what I meant," Po groaned.

Mr. Ping sighed. "I know it's not. I think it's time I told you something I should have told you a long time ago." He took a deep breath. "You might have been, kind of, a-a-adopted."

"I knew it!" Po cried.

Mr. Ping was surprised. "You knew? Who told you?"

"No one," Po admitted. "I mean, come on, Dad."

"But if you knew, why didn't you ever say anything?" his father asked.

"Why didn't *you* say anything?" Po replied. "How did I get here, Dad? Where did I come from?"

"Actually, you came from this," his father said softly.

He reached under the counter and pulled out a radish basket.

"It was just another day at the restaurant. Time to make the noodles," Mr. Ping began. "I went out to the back, where my vegetables had just been delivered. There were always cabbages, turnips, and radishes. Only there were no radishes. Just a very hungry baby panda."

Mr. Ping remembered how surprised he

had been at first. He looked around the alleys outside, but couldn't find anyone.

"There was no note. Of course, you could have eaten it," Mr. Ping pointed out. "I waited for someone to come looking for you, but no one did."

Mr. Ping smiled then, thinking about how cute Po had been. He could picture it like it was yesterday—luring the baby panda into the shop with a trail of dumplings. Po had gobbled up every one. "I brought you inside, fed you, gave you a bath, and fed you again," Mr. Ping explained. "And again. I even tried to put some pants on you. And then I made a decision that would change my life forever—to make my soup without radishes!"

Then Mr. Ping smiled again. "And to raise you as my own son. Xiao Po, my little panda. And from that moment on, both my soup and my life have been that much sweeter."

Po stared at the radish basket.

Mr. Ping wiped away a tear. "And, little Po, that is the end of the story." He sniffed.

"That's it?" Po asked. "That can't be it. There's gotta be more than that."

"Well, there was the time you ate all of my bamboo furniture," Mr. Ping replied. "It was imported, too."

A bunny appeared at the order window looking into the kitchen.

"One dumpling, please, Dragon Warrior size," he said.

Mr. Ping plucked a giant dumpling from the bubbling pot and put it in a basket. He handed it to the bunny, who stumbled under its weight. Then Mr. Ping turned back to his son.

"Oh, Po, your story may not have such a happy beginning, but look at how it turned out, hmm?" Mr. Ping pointed out. "You've got me, you've got kung fu, you've got noodles."

Po stood up, still holding the radish basket. "I know," he replied. "I just have questions. Like how did I fit in this tiny basket? Why didn't I like pants?"

He paused and gave a sad sigh. "And who am I?"

CHAPTER 5

"You Are No Match for Our Kung Fu"

Far from the Valley of Peace, Gongmen City was a sprawling metropolis. The busy shop-lined streets were crowded with villagers trading goods or searching for a bite of something delicious to eat.

Dominating the city was the ornate Peacock's Palace, with gleaming towers and turrets that rose gracefully into the clouds. Once, Lord and Lady Peacock had lived inside the Palace with their young son, Shen. But the peacock rulers left the Palace many years ago, and their son had been banished from Gongmen City forever.

When the peacocks gave up their thrones,

they turned the city over to the Kung Fu Council: Master Thundering Rhino, Master Storming Ox, and Master Croc—the strongest and wisest kung fu masters in the land. The peacocks' advisor, Soothsayer the goat, had stayed on to help them.

On this morning, Master Rhino sat on a dais in front of the Palace, watching Master Ox and Master Croc spar against each other. The old goat stood nearby, observing the morning activities.

Master Rhino coached his friends. "Good. Watch your form. Good. Better. Elbow! Straighten it out."

Master Ox struck a kung fu pose. "Watch this one!" he said confidently.

Suddenly, the Palace gates swung open. The two kung fu masters stopped their sparring as a white peacock with metal claws approached the masters.

Master Ox and Master Croc couldn't believe their eyes. "Shen?" they asked.

"Good afternoon, gentlemen," he said

coolly. "And now that we've gotten the pleasantries out of the way, please leave my house."

Master Ox's nostrils flared with anger. "*Your* house?" he asked.

"Yes. Didn't you see the peacock on the front door?" Shen asked. Then he spotted Soothsayer behind the platform. "Oh, there you are, Soothsayer. It seems your fortune-telling skills are not as good as you thought."

"We shall see, Shen," Soothsayer replied calmly.

Shen's eyes flashed with anger. "No, *you* shall see, you old goat!" Then he caught himself. "Where were we?"

Master Rhino, the eldest and largest of the masters, stood up.

"What do you want, Shen?"

"What is rightfully mine," the peacock replied. "Gongmen City."

"Gongmen City is under the stewardship of the Kung Fu Council and we will protect it," Rhino said firmly. "Even from you."

Shen laughed the kind of laugh that can send a chill up your spine. "I'm so glad you feel that way. Otherwise I'd have dragged *that* here for nothing."

An army of wolves poured through the gates, dragging a large wooden crate.

"What's in the box, Shen?" Master Ox asked.

"You want to see? It's a gift," Shen said, his voice dripping with fake sweetness. "It's your parting gift, in that it will part you. Part of you here, part of you there, and part of you way over there on that wall."

Master Ox stepped forward. "You insolent fool!"

He charged at Shen, and Master Croc leaped toward the peacock at the same time. Shen drew two long metal staffs from the sleeves of his cloak and moved quickly, striking both warriors at once. They staggered back, dazed from Shen's fast response.

Master Rhino swung his battle hammer—the blow sent the peacock flying across the room. His metal claws cut grooves in the ground as he skidded to a stop.

"Show-off," Shen said.

"That is a warning," Master Rhino said. "You are no match for my kung fu."

Shen grinned. "I agree. But this is."

He hopped on top of the wooden crate and it fell open. A black metal tube with a dragon's head on it was aimed right at Master Rhino.

Shen scraped his metal claw along the barrel of the cannon. Red-hot sparks shot up, igniting a fuse. Master Rhino watched helplessly as . . .

Kaboom!

CHAPTER 6

"Bring Lord Shen to Justice"

Back in the Valley of Peace, Po and the Furious Five were gathered around Master Shifu on the steps of the Jade Palace. Shifu was reading from a scroll he had just received from a messenger.

"Are you familiar with the Master of Gongmen City?" he asked.

"Master Thundering Rhino?" Po replied.

"Yes," said Shifu.

"Son of Legendary Flying Rhino?" Po asked.

"Yes!"

"And slayer of the Ten Thousand Serpents in the Valley of Woe?" Po asked.

"He's dead," Shifu told him.

Po's eyed widened. "Whoa."

"That's impossible," Tigress said. "Rhino's Iron Horn Defense is impervious to any technique."

"It was no technique," Shifu replied. "Lord Shen has created a weapon, one that breathes fire and spits metal. Unless he is stopped, this could be the end of kung fu."

"But I just *got* kung fu!" Po complained.

"And now you must save it," Shifu said. "Go. Destroy this weapon and bring Lord Shen to justice."

The Furious Five sprang past Shifu and made their way down the mountainside. Po hesitated.

"How can kung fu stop something that stops kung fu?" he asked Shifu.

"Remember, Dragon Warrior," Shifu replied. "If you are at peace, you can do anything."

Po leaped away and caught up to the Furious Five. They landed on the rooftops in the village down below. The villagers let out a cheer.

"Yay, Dragon Warrior!"

The hundreds of hopeful villagers made Po feel uneasy. What if he let them down? It's true, he had defeated Tai Lung, the evil snow leopard, and saved the Valley of Peace. But that was kung fu versus kung fu. This weapon—that was something else.

"Inner Peace, Inner Peace, Inner Peace," he chanted. He took a deep breath and let it out slowly.

"Po!" someone called.

Po looked down to see his dad standing on the ground below him.

"I got you a travel pack!" Mr. Ping called up.

Monkey liked the sound of that. "Oh, travel pack!"

Po jumped down from the rooftops and his friends followed. Mr. Ping handed a small sack to Monkey.

"Thanks, Dad," Po said.

"That's not *your* travel pack, son," said Mr. Ping.

He dragged a huge, heavy sack over to Po. "*This* is your travel pack. I packed you food for weeks. Cookies, buns, vegetables. I even packed all of your action figures."

He held up Po's action figures of the Furious Five. Po had played with the toys back when he had only been able to admire the kung fu masters from afar. Monkey laughed.

Po was embarrassed. "Oh, hey, I don't know what those are. Never seen them before in my life!"

Then he leaned over to Mr. Ping. "Dad! You got scratches on my Tigress," he whispered.

"I also packed the paintings of our best times together. Just in case you get lonely." Mr. Ping took out the pictures. "That's me and you making noodles. And that's me and you eating noodles. And that's me giving you a piggyback ride."

He held out a picture of himself squashed under the weight of a huge baby panda. "Look!

Isn't that cute? On second thought, I'll hang on to this one." He tucked the picture into his apron.

"Um . . ." Po was touched, but still embarrassed. "Listen, I gotta go."

"Of course, of course, you're the Dragon Warrior," Mr. Ping said, trying not to show how sad he was.

"Only if I save kung fu," Po said. "And if I don't . . . what am I?"

"You're my son," Mr. Ping said softly. Po looked away, and Mr. Ping suddenly felt worried. "Right?"

Tigress appeared next to Po. Strong, skilled, and smart, Tigress acted as leader of the Furious Five. And behind those sharp claws and gleaming fangs was a very kind heart.

"Po, it's time," she said.

Po nodded to his dad. "Uh, good-bye," he said. He turned and followed Monkey and the others as he walked away. Tigress hung back.

"Don't worry, Mr. Ping," Tigress assured

him. "He'll be back before you can say *noodles*."

Mr. Ping watched his son walk away.

"Noodles," he said softly.

38

CHAPTER 7

"I Am Not Freaking Out!"

It was a long journey to Gongmen City. Po and the Furious Five kept a quick pace as they crossed the Chinese countryside. They forged their way through snowy mountains and faced the heat of hot desert sand.

While they made their way to the city, Shen and his army of wolves had already begun their takeover. Master Ox and Master Croc left the Palace. Shen took his place on the throne his parents had given up years before. His wolf soldiers ran through the streets, stealing from the terrified citizens. They unloaded boats filled with metal and carted it to the Palace, where Shen was now in control of what he wanted: barrels and barrels of explosive black powder. The wolves brought the powder to the old fireworks factory.

Finally Po and the Furious Five reached the last leg of their journey: a river crossing. Night was falling as they made their way over the smooth water in a sampan—a narrow, flat-bottomed boat with a small cabin on board for sleeping. The boat captain steered the sampan through the water as Po and the Five settled in for the night.

Tigress, Viper, Monkey, Mantis, and Crane fell asleep easily. But Po tossed and turned. In a brief period of fitful sleep, he began to dream . . .

Po walked across the plains. In the distance, he saw two pandas. He knew they were his mother and father.

"Mom? Dad? Is that you?" He ran after them. "Mom! Dad!"

"Hey, son. You're back," said his father.

"Honey, what are you doing here?" asked his mother.

Po was confused. "Huh? But I thought—"

"We replaced you, dear," said his mother. "With this lovely radish."

Po realized that his mom was cradling a white radish in her arms like a baby.

"What?" Po asked, horrified.

"It's quiet, polite, and, frankly, does better kung fu," his dad told him.

The radish leaped onto the ground and started doing some impressive kung fu moves.

"No, no, no!" Po cried. "Wait!"

The radish jumped onto Po, knocking him onto the ground. Then it began to furiously pound Po.

"Finish him!" Po's panda dad yelled.

The radish leaped up and hurtled toward Po once more. Then everything went black. A red eye appeared in the darkness, and Po screamed . . .

He sat up, wide awake and terrified. Then he took a deep breath.

It was only a dream. With a sigh, Po crawled out of the cabin. He anxiously paced the deck of the sampan.

"Radish, radish, radish," he mumbled.

He stormed over to the ship's mast and gave it an angry punch. *"Hiyah!"*

Fat drops of water from the sail above plopped onto his head. At first Po just felt annoyed. But then he remembered Master Shifu's teaching. He needed to find his Inner Peace. He closed his eyes and started to slowly move his arms.

"Inner Pea—"

Plop! Another drop fell on his head.

"Pea—"

Plop!

"Pea—"

Plop! Plop! Plop!

"Aaaargh!" Po cried. Angry, he punched the mast over and over again. A deluge of drops poured down on his head.

More frustrated than ever, Po beat his head against the mast. "Inner! Peace! Inner! Peace! Inner Peace Inner Peace Inner Peace Inner Peace!"

"Ahem."

Po stopped what he was doing and turned

to see Tigress standing on the cabin.

"Oh, I'm uh, training," Po replied, embarrassed.

"The mast is not a worthy opponent," Tigress said. She leaped onto the deck and held out her hand with the palm facing up.

"I am ready," she said solemnly.

"Um, okay," Po said. He reared back and punched Tigress's palm as hard as he could. Her arm didn't budge one bit.

"Oowwwww!" Po cried, holding his hurt hand. "I think I prefer the mast."

"I used to punch the ironwood trees by the Palace to train," Tigress explained. "Now I feel nothing."

Po sighed. "That's severely cool."

A hint of a smile appeared on Tigress's face. She held out her palm once more. "Again."

Po gave it his best shot. *"Hi-yah!"*

This time, it hurt a little less. Po and Tigress sparred, trading blows.

"So, uh, this punching ironwood trees. How long did you have to do that?" Po asked.

"Twenty years," Tigress replied.

"Twenty years?" Po frowned. "Is there any, you know, faster way? You know, until you don't feel anything?"

"No," Tigress said, dodging to the side. "Besides—"

She grabbed Po's arm as he swung at her again, then flipped him.

Slam! Po collided hard with the deck.

"I don't think Hard Style is . . . your thing," she said.

Tigress knelt down next to him. "Po, why are you *really* out here?"

"I just found out that my dad isn't really my dad," Po said sadly.

Tigress raised an eyebrow. "Your dad . . . the goose?"

Po nodded.

"That must have been quite a shock," Tigress said.

"Yeah," Po answered.

"And this bothers you?" his friend asked.

"Are you kidding me?" Po sat up. "We're

warriors, right? Nerves of steel! Souls of platinum! Like you. So hard core you don't feel anything."

Tigress was surprised. Did Po really think that? Before she could ask him, Mantis came out of the cabin.

"So what are you guys talking about?" Mantis asked.

"Nothing. Nothing!" Po said quickly.

The rest of the Five came out onto the deck, too. They had heard everything.

"Po's having daddy issues," Viper said.

"Man, I'm so lucky!" Mantis said. The little green warrior hopped up on Po's knee. "I don't have any problems with my dad. Maybe it's because Mom ate his head before I was born. I don't know."

"Mantis, this isn't about you," Viper scolded. "Po is the one freaking out."

"I am *not* freaking out!" Po protested.

"Po," Tigress interrupted.

"I'm freaking *in*!" Po insisted.

"Po," Tigress said calmly.

Po turned around. "What?"

"We're here."

Behind her, they saw Gongmen City in the distance.

CHAPTER 8

"Find This Panda and Bring Him to Me!"

Beautiful tapestries hung in the tower of Peacock's Palace in Gongmen City. Lord and Lady Peacock's proud faces looked down on their loyal subjects.

Rip!

Two gorillas tore the tapestries from the ceiling and dropped them in a heap on the floor. Then, with the help of the wolf soldiers, they rolled the cannon over the pile.

Lord Shen watched his army with pride. If only his parents could see him now, they never would have underestimated their son or banished him from his home.

The sun glinted off the top of an ornate

throne in the center of the room. "Ahh, my father's throne," Shen said as he walked toward it. "How I've waited for this moment."

Shen motioned to one of the gorillas. The guard lumbered over and lifted the throne, then heaved it out the window.

Then the gorillas wheeled the cannon to the center of the room where the throne once stood.

"A little to the left," Shen directed.

"But it's so heavy," one of the guards complained.

Shen narrowed his eyes at the gorilla. "I've waited thirty years to reclaim Gongmen City," he said. "Everything must be exactly how I envisioned it. And I envisioned it a little to the left!"

The gorillas scrambled to move the cannon. They grunted as they pushed and pulled. Finally they looked to Shen for approval.

The peacock nodded. "Perfect," he said. "With the weapon by my side . . ." He paused and considered the position of the cannon again. He looked at the gorillas. "A little bit more."

The guards went back to the cannon and pushed some more. It rolled into place, and, at last, Lord Shen was pleased.

"All of China will bow before me!" Shen cried, his voice echoing around the tower. "We move out in three days when the moon is full and the tide is high," he told his team.

Then the peacock turned to Soothsayer. She was sitting in a corner of the tower room.

"Why don't you tell me my fortune *now*, you silly old goat?" Shen taunted. "Tell me the glorious future that awaits me!"

Soothsayer nodded. "Come closer, and I will show you," she said.

Shen walked up to Soothsayer and stood in front of her.

"Closer . . . ," Soothsayer said.

Shen took another few steps. He looked at the goat carefully.

"Closer, closer," Soothsayer said.

The peacock moved so close, he had to bend down so he was eye to eye with Soothsayer.

She leaned in and began to nibble on Shen's long, flowing robes.

Shen yanked them back in disgust. "That is the finest silk in the province, not a snack!" he yelled.

Soothsayer pulled a single thread from between her teeth. She dropped it into a bowl with some other objects. She snapped her fingers, and a flash of green light appeared.

"What do you see?" Shen asked, curious.

"A peacock," Soothsayer replied.

A cloud of smoke rose from the bowl in the shape of a peacock. Shen smiled.

"Being stopped by a warrior of black and white," Soothsayer continued.

Shen was furious. He released the blades from his robes and struck the bowl, shattering it. "It's impossible and you know it," he said.

But the wise old goat knew better. "It is not impossible and *he* knows it." She pointed behind Shen.

The peacock turned around. There was no one there.

Suddenly, the door burst open, and the leader of the wolves bounded into the room. "Lord Shen!" he cried. "I saw a panda! It fought like a demon. Black and white, big and furry, soft and squishy."

Shen narrowed his eyes at the wolf. "There are no more pandas," he said.

Soothsayer looked at Shen. "Even with his poor eyesight he can see the truth. Why is it that you cannot?"

"Find this panda and bring him to me!" Shen yelled.

The wolf leader took off.

Shen approached Soothsayer once again. "So one panda lives," he said. "That does not make you right."

"You're right," Soothsayer agreed. "Being *right* makes me right."

Shen glared out the window at the city below. "Then I will kill him and prove you wrong."

Suddenly, he heard a strange noise. He turned to see the goat chewing on his robes.

"Will you stop that!" he yelled. He yanked the silk out of her mouth.

CHAPTER 9

"Stop That Costume!"

Over at the harbor, the sampan boat slid onto shore. Po and the Furious Five leaped off of the ship and ran into the city. They climbed to the nearest rooftop and looked out over Gongmen City. Po narrated their every move.

"As the brave warriors scaled the rooftop to scope out the land, questions burned unanswered. Will they find the secret hidden lair of Shen and his diabolical weapon? Will they—"

Po stopped when he spotted the tall Peacock's Palace in the distance.

"Oh. Right. Yes!" he continued. "The

answer is yes! Our heroes make a plan—to march into the tower and proclaim, 'We are the Dragon Warrior and the Furious Five, and we are here to bring you to justice!'"

Po started to leap off of the roof, but Mantis yanked him back.

"What are you doing? This place is crawling with wolves," he said.

A small army of wolf guards swarmed the streets. They followed their leader, who wore a red eye symbol on his uniform.

A vision flashed before Po's eyes . . . a red eye . . . a baby's cries.

"It's him!" Po realized.

"Isn't that the guy who hammered you in the face?" Crane asked.

"I do not like that guy," Po said.

Tigress pulled him back from the roof's edge. "If those wolves spot us, we'll lose the element of surprise."

"And then we'll end up just like Master Rhino," Monkey added.

Tigress was firm. "We're going to have to

do this quietly. That means no marching, no proclaiming—and no kung fu." She gave Po a hard look.

Po thought about this for a moment. Then he opened his mouth to speak, but Tigress was one step ahead.

"Belly bumps and butt smashes count as kung fu."

Po nodded obediently. "Got it. Stealth mode."

They left the rooftop and began to cautiously make their way through the city. As kung fu masters, the Furious Five knew how to move carefully and quietly without being noticed.

But Po was not as skilled in the art of stealth. He tried his best, but he accidentally bumped into a fruit cart. Po caught the fruit as it fell, juggling it.

"Whew!" Po said. He took a step backward and, this time, knocked over a noodle stand! Slippery noodles spilled out onto the street. A pig slipped on the noodles and collided with a pot seller's cart, and the metal pots banged together like gongs. Within seconds the busy street was in chaos.

The wolf guards started questioning everyone.

"All right, what happened here?" a guard asked a frightened bunny.

In the chaos, the wolves didn't see Po.

"Misdirection," Po said proudly as he slipped away.

The Furious Five moved back to the safety of the rooftops before the chaos hit. Tigress noticed the commotion below.

"Where's Po?" she asked.

Then they spotted something in the crowd. A giant dragon costume weaved its way through the busy street. Two furry legs and one round belly stuck out from under the costume.

Po searched for the Five, but he couldn't see anything from underneath the costume. He bumped right into a fireworks stand, setting it on fire. Po didn't even know what he had done.

The Five left the roof and quickly joined Po under the costume.

"So that was stealth mode, eh?" Crane asked.

Po shrugged. "To be honest, not one of my stronger modes."

They made their way through the city streets inside the dragon costume. Through the fabric, they could hear wolf guards harassing the citizens.

One wolf was terrorizing an innocent sheep.

"Hey, you! This rice is raw!" the soldier yelled.

"But you stole all of my metal pots for Lord Shen!" the sheep protested.

"Either you cook my rice, or I cook you," the wolf threatened.

"Po, do something!" Crane hissed.

"How am I supposed to help her cook rice without getting caught?" Po wondered. "Wait—I have a better idea."

He brought the dragon up behind the wolf. Po reached through the mouth and punched the wolf. Then he yanked him inside the costume.

Pow! Bam! Wham! Whack! Slam! The Furious Five took care of the wolf and kicked him out of the back of the costume. He landed with a thud in the grass.

A bunny passing by gasped at the sight of the wolf-eating dragon. But the sheep was grateful.

"Oh, thank you so much!" the sheep said. "Who are you?"

"We're here to liberate the city and bring Shen to justice," Po told her.

The sheep nervously looked around. "You will need help."

"Thank you, brave sheep, but it is too dangerous," Po said bravely. "I cannot let you—"

"No, not me," the sheep said. She lowered her voice. "It's not safe to speak here."

"Right," Po agreed.

He quickly pulled the sheep under the costume. To the bunny, it looked like the dragon was having a sheep for dessert! The bunny fled in terror.

Inside the costume, Po spoke to the sheep.

"Don't worry, no one can see us," Po explained. "We're in stealth mode."

"I'm talking about Masters Ox and Croc," the sheep said.

"What? They're still alive?" Po asked. "Where can we find them?"

"Shen locked them up. They're in the Gongmen Jail."

The sheep hurried out of the dragon costume.

"Thanks, sheep!" Po called after her.

The wolf that the dragon had "eaten" earlier got back on his feet, dazed. He spotted the dragon costume hurrying away.

"Hey! Stop that costume!" he yelled.

"Get them!" cried the wolf leader.

A group of wolves charged after the

costume, circling the dragon.

"Now! Gotcha!" the wolf leader shouted.

The wolves pierced their swords through the fabric. They ripped off the costume . . . only to find fruit crates underneath.

"Huh?" The guard was confused. "Spread out and search everywhere!"

"What about over there?" another guard asked, pointing.

"Is *there* a part of everywhere?" the first guard asked.

"I . . . I guess," said the second guard.

"Then search there!" the wolf guard barked.

Besides stealth, speed was another specialty of the Furious Five. Before the wolves could catch them, they'd slipped out of the costume and hidden under some large barrels. When the wolf guards passed, they popped out.

They'd ended up in a dark alleyway full of spooky shadows.

"They must be close," Po remarked. "I can feel a kung fu chill rising up my spine."

Viper slithered out of Po's barrel. "Sorry, Po, that's just me."

Tigress looked down the alley and pointed to a sign. "There it is. Gongmen Jail."

CHAPTER 10

"You Are the Warrior of Black and White!"

Two wolf guards stood sentry in front of the entrance to the jail. A tiny barrel rolled in front of them, stopping right at their feet. The guards bent down, curious—and Mantis jumped out of the barrel!

"Hi-yaaaaaah!" The powerful insect easily flipped each of the wolves, slamming them into each other. Now it was safe for Po and the Furious Five to enter the jail.

They walked down a hallway to a balcony that looked down on the jail cells below. There were no guards around, but still, they knew they had to be careful.

"At the first sign of wolves I'll give you the

signal," Monkey said. *"Kaka! Ki! Ki!"*

"You mean like Crane does?" Po asked.

"Why don't I just give the signal?" Crane asked.

Monkey shrugged. "I sound more authentic."

Po peered over the balcony and spotted a shadow with two horns coming from one of the cells. He gasped.

"What is it?" Tigress asked.

"Look, look, look!" Po said. "There he is! I can't believe I'm about to fight side by side with Master Storming Ox. I want to take a moment to enjoy the anticipation."

Po took a deep breath and closed his eyes. His face turned pink and then bright red.

"Po, breathe," Tigress said.

Po exhaled, and he and Tigress jumped down to the floor below. They walked up to the cell holding Master Ox and Master Croc. Master Ox was all bulk and muscle, but there was agility and skill behind that raw power. Master Croc had intelligent, reptilian eyes and carried two long swords as sharp as the fangs in his snout.

"Master Ox! Master Croc! We're the Dragon Warrior and the Furious Five," Po said.

"We have come from the Valley of Peace to stop Shen and his weapon," Tigress added.

"But first we need to free you from this cell," Po said. He grabbed two of the iron bars and tried to pull them apart. "I got it . . . I got it . . . *grrrrr!* Any second now . . . in a minute . . . I didn't have a very big breakfast. I'm a lot stronger when I have my protein."

Tigress stepped back and aimed a kick at the cell door. It crashed down.

"Come on, you guys!" Po said urgently. "Yeah! We're coming for you, Shen! Woohoo!"

Po ran toward the exit—and then realized that nobody was following him. He walked back to the cell.

"What's going on? Guys, are we going or not?" he asked. "Do you want us to meet you there later? I mean, you do want to take back your city, right?"

"It's too late for that," Master Ox said sadly. He and Master Croc picked up the cell door and put it back on its hinges. They sat in their cell, looking out at Po and the Five.

"No it's not!" Po protested. "Not if we all work together!"

He yanked off the cell door, but Master Ox grabbed it back from him.

"Shen put us in here, and here we stay," Master Ox said firmly.

Po couldn't believe it. "You are the Kung Fu Council! You were entrusted to protect the citizens of Gongmen City!"

"*Were* the Kung Fu Council," Master Ox corrected him.

Po grabbed the cell door again. Master Croc grabbed it back. The three warriors went back and forth with the door as they argued.

"Oh, so you're in the Council only as long as there is no danger involved?" Po asked.

Master Ox's nostrils flared with anger.

"You don't know what you're talking about, kid!"

Po threw the cell door aside, and it broke into pieces.

"Master Ox, your dedication to justice liberated the village of Shu Mai!" he said, pointing to the powerful warrior.

Master Ox responded by kicking up two iron bars from the floor, sending them flying at Po. Po pushed the bars away with his paws and dodged a blow from Master Ox. Then he faced Master Croc.

"And Croc, your blades silenced the badger bandits who talked about your mom!"

"A warrior's greatest honor is his mother," Master Croc replied.

"Honor? If Master Thundering Rhino could see you now!" Po said angrily.

Master Ox advanced on Po with a flurry of moves.

"You weren't there! You don't understand what you're up against! A lifetime of training and dedication gone in an instant. His kung fu was powerless against Shen."

Master Ox dropped the iron bars, and a look of great sadness crossed his face as he remembered his lost friend. "And when the smoke cleared, all that was left of Master Rhino was his war hammer."

Po thought about this. "So the weapon can't destroy hammers?"

"No, no," Master Croc replied. "You see, he was holding it to the side, like this, I guess. It must have missed his hammer. But that's not the point, anyway!"

"Unless you want the city to suffer, the only honorable thing to do is surrender," Master Ox said.

"Or leave," Master Croc answered.

"Yes, he is right. I suppose you could also leave," agreed Master Ox.

Po was speechless. He shook his fist at Master Ox.

"Come on, Po," Tigress said. "Let's just go."

Po glared at Master Ox and Master Croc. "You stay in your prison of fear with bars made of hopelessness. And all you get are three square meals a day of shame! We'll take on Shen and prove to all those who are hungry for justice and honor that kung fu still lives!"

"Yeah!"

Po turned and saw one lonely prisoner in his cell.

Suddenly the door to the jail burst open. The wolf leader and his soldiers flooded into the room.

Po looked around. What had happened to his warning?

"Monkey?" he called out.

"Kaka!" Monkey replied.

"Found you, panda!" the wolf leader cried.

"You!" Po said.

The Furious Five sprang into action.

Bam! Slam! Wham! The wolf soldiers didn't stand a chance.

Suddenly the wolf leader was left facing off with Po and the Five alone.

"Uh oh," he said.

Po stared the wolf leader down. "You're mine!" he growled.

The wolf leader fled the jail.

Po turned to the Five. "Let's kick some butt!"

CHAPTER 11

"Hang On!"

The wolf leader ran out into the street and hopped into a rickshaw, a two-wheeled cart pulled by a pig.

"Get me to the Palace!" the wolf leader yelled.

"Yes, sir!" the driver replied, and the rickshaw took off.

"Stop him! Ya!" Mantis cried.

The Furious Five left Po behind and chased after the rickshaw.

"Faster!" Monkey yelled.

Suddenly Po sailed over their heads. He was sitting inside his own rickshaw, but no one was pulling him. His extra weight was enough to send the rickshaw speeding down the cobblestone slope.

"Yeeeeehaaaaa!" Po yelled.

Monkey cheered him on. "Yeah! Go! Go!"

The wolf leader growled at his rickshaw driver. "Lose him!"

"Yes, sir," replied the pig, puffing and panting.

Then the driver saw his chance. He quickly steered the rickshaw to the right and headed down an alley. Po was going too fast to make the turn.

"Viper!" Po yelled.

"Hang on!" Viper called back.

She sailed through the air, snagging the handle of Po's rickshaw with her tail. Then she whipped to the right, sending Po into the turn.

"Ya ha!" Po cheered.

Furious, the wolf leader grabbed his poor rickshaw driver and tossed him aside. Po frantically steered to the left to avoid hitting the helpless pig.

71

"Uncool! *Very* uncool!" Po shouted to the wolf leader.

"Nope. This is uncool!" the wolf replied.

He grabbed a goose then a bunny then a pig and tossed them one by one at Po's rickshaw. Po knew he couldn't steer out of the way fast enough.

"Guys, guys, guys!" he yelled.

The Five backed up Po, pulling the helpless pedestrians out of the way. But the wolf leader wasn't finished. With an evil look, he held up a basket of crying baby bunnies.

"No, no!" Po pleaded.

The wolf tossed the baby bunnies at Po. They slammed into his face, covering his eyes.

"Ha ha! So long, Dragon Loser!" the wolf cackled.

At the end of the alley, workers had built two levels of scaffolding in front of a building that needed repair. Bamboo poles supported each level of boards.

The wolf steered his rickshaw onto the

first level. But Po couldn't see. His rickshaw soared up a wooden ramp onto the second level of boards.

"Cute bunnies, off the face! Excuse me!" Po cried frantically.

The last bunny hopped to the safety of Po's shoulder. Now Po could see what lay ahead— and it wasn't good. The platform ended abruptly in front of them. In seconds, they would go crashing to the street below.

Po lowered his foot and braked with all his might, steering the rickshaw onto a roof. The baby bunnies screamed as the out-of-control cart hurtled along the rooftop. The Furious Five raced along the streets below, searching for Po.

"We've lost them!" Tigress said.

The rickshaw soared over the rooftop. The baby bunnies tumbled through the air. Luckily the rickshaw landed on two lantern ropes strung over the street, attached to two poles. Po jumped out of the rickshaw and then bounced on the ropes. The baby bunnies landed safely in the empty cart.

"*Wheeee!*" the bunnies cried. "Again! Again!"

The rickshaw sped along the ropes, heading for a brick wall.

"Uh oh," Po said. "Crane, catch!"

He grabbed the poles and swung down, kicking the ropes. The baby bunnies bounced into the air once more. Crane swooped down and caught them safely.

"Gotcha!" Crane said.

The rickshaw slammed into the brick wall, shattering into pieces. Po landed on the street, still clutching one of the bamboo poles. The pole stuck into one of the loose rickshaw wheels, and Po rode the wheel down the street, still chasing the wolf. But the leader was too far ahead.

"Guys, guys, guys! Give me a shove!" Po called out.

"Mantis, now!" Tigress said.

"Ya!" With a cry, Mantis grabbed Tigress and flung her forward. As she sailed through the air, she concentrated on gathering her chi—the life force inside her body. Controlling chi was a skill every kung fu master had to learn, and Tigress had learned it well.

"Heeee yaaaaah!"

She connected with Po in an explosion of chi energy. Po shot forward with rocket speed. He flew off his wheel and landed in the rickshaw with the wolf leader. They started to grapple, each one trying to toss out the other one.

"Is that all you got?" the wolf leader said. "'Cause it feels like I'm fighting a big ol' fluffy cloud."

Po looked up the street. He saw a row of low-hanging signs coming up fast.

"Well," Po said, "this cloud is about to bring the thunder."

He quickly ducked, and the first sign smacked the wolf leader right in the face.

"Ow! Ow! Ow!"

Groggy, the wolf leader fell back. He knocked into Po, causing the panda to flip up. Now it was Po's turn to get smacked by the signs.

"Ow! Why! Are! There! So! Many! Signs!"

"Ha! Ha!" laughed the wolf leader.

"Come here!" Po cried.

Bam! Po landed on top of the wolf as they hit the ground in a cloud of dust.

CHAPTER 12

"We Surrender!"

Po stood over the defeated wolf leader.

"Yeah! Taste the defeat! The next time you mess with a panda, you better bring the whole . . . army."

Po looked up and saw that they had landed right in front of the Palace gates. A huge army of growling wolves and massive gorillas surrounded them. Each one had a crossbow trained on Po.

The Furious Five jumped down to help Po, but the guards quickly captured them. The wolf leader stood up, brushed himself off, and gave a satisfied chuckle.

"Guess nobody told you—if you mess with

the wolf, you get the fangs," the wolf leader said. Then he hit Po in the belly.

Po doubled over, and the wolf leader grinned.

"What are you gonna do now?" he asked.

Po's eyes narrowed with steely determination, like he was about to fight. Instead he threw up his hands.

"We surrender!"

The wolves descended on the team, roughly binding them in shackles and chains.

"You can chain my body," Crane began proudly, "but you will never chain my—" A wolf shackled his skinny neck. "—warrior spirit," he finished, his voice muffled.

Po held up Mantis. "Hey, don't forget the little guy," he told the guards.

Mantis frowned. "Did you just call me—"

A wolf grabbed Mantis out of Po's paw and stuffed him in a small cage.

"Po, what are you doing?" Tigress whispered.

"Trust me," he said quietly. "I got—ow!"

The wolf leader slapped shackles on Po's wrists.

"Ow!" Po complained. Then he looked down at the cuffs and a look of excitement lit up his face. "Eight point acupressure system cuffs! Wow! Just like the ones that held Tai Lung. The more you move, the tighter they get."

The gorilla guard yanked Po by the shackles.

"Oof! These are the best cuffs!" Po cried.

Inside Peacock's Palace, Shen waited anxiously to meet his foe. He gazed into the mirror, imagining he was addressing the black-and-white warrior.

"Greetings, panda. We meet at last."

But the reflection in the mirror didn't look menacing enough.

"No, no, no, no, no," Shen clucked. He turned away and then dramatically turned back to the mirror.

"Greetings, panda. We at last meet," he said with a wave of his wing. "Yes!"

In the mirror's reflection, he noticed Soothsayer watching him. He cleared his throat, embarrassed. "Yes, that's it. Perfect."

"You are afraid for a reason," the old goat said.

"I am not afraid," Shen replied. "I am just being a gracious host."

Outside, Shen's guards dragged Po and the Furious Five through the Palace's gates. Heavily armed wolves and gorillas glared down at them from the top of the tower.

Tigress whispered to Po. "I hope this turns out better than that plan to cook rice in your stomach by eating it raw and then drinking boiling water."

"This plan is nothing like that," Po replied.

"How?" Tigress asked.

Po's eyes gleamed. "Because this one's gonna work."

They suddenly stopped short at the edge of a huge crater in the center of the courtyard. Master Rhino's battle hammer was mounted on a pillar in the center—a reminder to all of the power of Shen's cannon. Po and Tigress gasped at the sight.

The wolf leader laughed. "Keep moving."

Shen and Soothsayer watched the procession from the tower balcony.

"He's bigger than I expected," Shen admitted. "Still, he arrives in chains, so all is well."

"Yes, all is well," Soothsayer said.

Shen was suddenly suspicious. "What do you mean, 'all is well'?"

"I'm simply agreeing with you," Soothsayer said innocently.

"But did you mean all is well from my point of view, or all is well from your point of view?" Shen asked.

Soothsayer considered this. "Well . . ."

"Well?" Shen asked impatiently.

"Well . . ."

"Well?!" Shen felt ready to explode.

"Well from the point of the universe," Soothsayer said finally.

"Bah!" Shen snorted. "Come. Let us receive our guests."

He walked off of the balcony, and Soothsayer reluctantly followed him.

CHAPTER 13

"The Beast of Gongmen Is the Future!"

The soldiers marched Po and the Furious Five inside the Palace. Po still carried Mantis's cage in his shackled paws. He gazed at the long staircase that zigzagged up to the throne room at the top of the tower.

"Ah, my old enemy . . . stairs."

Upstairs, Shen waited anxiously for his nemesis to walk through the door. Finally he heard massive footsteps approaching.

Boom! Boom! Boom!

A hulking shadow appeared in the stairwell, sending a shiver of fear through Shen.

Then a gorilla guard stepped into the room, carrying an exhausted Po on his back.

The guard dumped Po onto the floor with a thud.

"Ugh," Po said to the guard. "I threw up a little on the third landing. Whew! Maybe on the twelfth, too."

Shen cast Soothsayer a triumphant glance. Did she really think this clumsy thing could defeat him?

Shen cleared his throat. "Greetings, panda. At—"

"Hey, how you doin'?" Po interrupted.

"Hey," Shen replied.

Soothsayer walked up to Po. She looked him over from head to toe. Then she prodded him with her staff.

"You've grown up bigger than I thought," she said. "Strong. Healthy."

Po looked confused. "Look," he said. "I don't know who you are, but please stand aside, sir."

"That's a lady," Viper hissed from behind Po.

The panda did a double take. "Oh!

Sorry. The beard threw me. It's kind of misleading."

"Enough of this nonsense!" Shen cried. "Bring the prisoners—whom I have at last met—to me," he told the guards.

The guards pulled Po and the Five closer to Shen.

"Get ready, guys," Po told the Five. "Keep your eyes peeled for the . . . weapon!"

Po leaped at the cannon. "Spear kick!" The cannon split into tiny pieces. "Yes! We did it! I just kung fu'd it! You guys see that?"

Po turned to see everyone staring at him. He was standing beside the cannon. The weapon towered over him. He looked at the floor where pieces of a model lay at his feet.

Shen laughed. "Do you really think that this is the warrior destined to defeat me?" he asked Soothsayer. "A lifetime to plot his revenge, and he comes to me on his knees."

"A lifetime?" Po asked. "We only heard about Master Rhino a few days ago, and we came to avenge him!"

Soothsayer gave Po a long, hard look. "You've come to avenge nothing else?"

"And all the pots and pans you stole and melted down for that weapon," Po said to Shen.

"Nothing else?" Soothsayer prodded further.

Po thought about it. "Well . . . Master Ox and Master Croc, I guess," he said. "But they're not exactly dead. Why? Is there something else?"

"What?" Shen said with a laugh. "Everyone here but you knows?"

"Okay," Po said. "You guys are really confusing. First the weapon is tiny, then it's big. Then the goat is a lady but has a beard. I say we drop all the pleasantries and settle this."

A blade shot out of Shen's sleeve and he aimed it at Po. "The only reason you're still alive is that I find your stupidity mildly amusing."

"Well I find your evilness extremely

annoying," Po challenged.

"Who do you think you are, panda?" Shen said.

"Who do *you* think I am?" Po replied.

Shen and Po stared each other down. Finally Shen directed the gorillas, "Take aim!"

The cannon pointed at Po and the Five.

Po winked at Tigress and nodded to the cage he was carrying with Mantis inside. Now Tigress could see that it wasn't Mantis at all—it was Po's Mantis action figure! Maybe Po had a plan after all.

"Fire!" Shen yelled.

The gorilla lit the fuse. Shen watched with glee.

Suddenly Mantis zipped in and put out the flame. He was gone again before anyone saw him.

"I said light it!" Shen demanded.

The gorilla looked confused. But he lit the fuse again.

Then Shen saw something over the top of the cannon. It was Mantis! Shen turned to Po.

He realized that the Mantis in the cage was just a fake.

"Get the cannon!" Po called as Tigress was released from her chains.

Tigress freed Po and the rest of the Five. They quickly leaped into action, taking out the shocked wolf guards before they knew what hit them. But the fuse on the cannon was burning faster and faster.

"Tigress!" Po called out.

Tigress jumped up and kicked the cannon with all of her might. It flipped through the air, landing on its barrel.

Boom! The cannonball shot right through the floor.

Mantis delivered a powerful kick, smashing the cannon through the hole. It tumbled through the tower, smashing into stairs and railings as it fell.

"*Sheeeeennnnnnn!*" Po tackled Shen, wrestling him to the ground. Shen spread his white tail feathers. On top of each one was a marking that looked exactly like a red eye.

A vision passed before Po's eyes. Po's mother, holding a radish. Hot flames leaped up all around him—and in the center of it all was Shen.

Po jumped up with a cry, freeing Shen.

"Po, what are you doing?" Tigress asked.

"You! You were there!" Po pointed at Shen.

Shen understood. "Yes. And so were you."

He smiled and hurled four sharp blades at Po. Snarling, Tigress slashed them back with her sharp claws.

Shen jumped out of the balcony widow. Tigress raced past a dazed Po to the balcony's edge. The others followed. They looked over the edge to see the peacock flying toward the fireworks factory on the horizon.

Soothsayer watched, horrified. But there was nothing she could do. A gorilla guard snatched her up and whisked her away.

CHAPTER 14

"The Only Way Out Is Up!"

Tigress turned to Po, fuming. "You just let Shen get away!"

"At least we destroyed the cannon," Mantis pointed out.

Boom! Boom! Boom! From the balcony, they could see flashes of flame bursting from the fireworks factory in the distance.

"Oh. No, he's got way more," Mantis said.

Cannonballs soared through the air, aimed right at the tower.

Kaboom! The tower shook as the cannonballs made contact. Chunks of stone and other debris rained down on them.

"Aaaaaah!" Po cried out as they all dodged

the falling missiles.

Kaboom! Another cannonball hit.

Po raced across the trembling floor toward the balcony.

"Watch out!" Tigress warned.

Po tumbled through a gaping hole in the floor, but Viper was right on him. She wrapped her tail around his foot, saving him just in time.

"Urg! Help me up!" Viper said with a grunt.

"No, get him down! Use the ropes!" Tigress urged.

"Okay!" Po replied.

Po and the Five leaped down the tower shaft onto ropes lined with dangling Chinese lanterns. They slid down the ropes to the floor below.

Boom! Boom! Boom! More cannonballs blasted the tower. The tall structure began to sway and groan. Po and the Five raced toward the main entrance of the Palace, but a lower balcony gave way outside. It crashed in front of the entrance, blocking the way out.

"We're trapped!" Po yelled.

"This way!" Tigress cried.

As they reached the top, Tigress kicked a hole in the wall. They leaped out onto a roof. Down below, the wolf guards were loading their bows with flaming arrows.

"Fire!" the wolf leader commanded.

"Get back!" Tigress warned as the fiery missiles whizzed toward them. Tigress blocked them skillfully.

She quickly assessed the situation. It was a short drop down to the ground, but there were too many wolf guards to count. Above them, the tower swayed, and Tigress was sure it would fall any minute.

That gave her an idea.

"The only way out is up!"

"What?" her team members asked.

Tigress didn't answer—there wasn't time. She and Po ran up the side of the toppling tower followed by the rest of the Five.

While the Furious Five and Po tried to

Po and the Furious Five

Wolf bandits invade a mountain village while
innocent bunnies and pigs look on in terror.

Po faces off against Boss Wolf.

Lord Shen vows to rule China with the help of his wolf and gorilla army.

Baby Po tumbles out of a radish basket and into
Mr. Ping's noodle shop.

Mr. Ping feeds and feeds his new son.

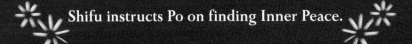
Shifu instructs Po on finding Inner Peace.

Lord Shen takes over Gongmen City with the help of his secret weapon—a cannon.

Po and the Furious Five enter Peacock's Palace as prisoners.

Po discovers that Shen was there the night his parents abandoned him.

Soothsayer helps Po remember his past and find peace.

escape, Shen was stationed safely in the abandoned fireworks factory. He watched them, amazed.

Where are they going? he wondered.

"To the top!" Tigress called out as they ran.

"Come on! Keep going!" Viper urged.

They reached the top of the tower just as it crashed to the ground—exactly as Tigress had planned.

"Here we go!" Po called out.

They all jumped at once, sailing over the heads of the guards—and clearing the Palace gates.

Boom! The tower slammed down behind them, but they were safe. They disappeared into the city streets, dodging flaming arrows as they ran.

CHAPTER 15

"I Have To Find Out What Happened!"

Shen was furious that Po and the Furious Five had escaped.

"You idiot!" Shen smacked his gorilla gunner right in the face.

"Ow! My nose!" the gorilla whined.

Shen climbed down from the cannon platform, followed by the wolf leader. All of the stolen metal had been melted down and used to make cannons—lots of them. And now it was time to use them.

"Assemble the wolf army!" Shen commanded. "I want them ready to move! The Year of the Peacock begins now!"

The wolf leader spoke up. "Actually, sir,

this is really the Year of the Rabbit. There is no peacock." Then he looked at Shen's angry face and corrected himself. "Oh, this is the Year of the Peacock, of course!"

Shen just stared at him. "Get the wolves ready . . . now!" he demanded angrily. "Now! Now! Now! Now! Now!"

The wolf leader scampered away. "Move! Move! Move! Move! Move!" he told his soldiers.

The wolves scrambled around the factory, getting things ready for Shen's massive invasion. One of the wolves let out a loud howl.

The signal carried all the way to the center of Gongmen City. Hundreds of wolf guards followed the signal, racing across the rooftops to get to the factory.

Po and the Five quickly made their way through the city, keeping to the shadows. They soon arrived back at Gongmen City Jail.

Po tumbled down the steps and landed on

the dusty floor. Tigress got in his face.

"You had Shen. What happened?" she asked.

"What are you talking about?" Po asked innocently. "I don't know what you're talking about. I . . . yeah, okay, he caught me off guard."

"The truth," Tigress demanded.

Po refused to answer.

"Fine," Tigress said. She motioned to Master Ox and Master Croc, still in their jail cell. "They will keep you far from danger."

"Real far," Master Croc promised.

"What?" Po asked.

"You're staying here," Tigress said firmly. She started to walk to the door, and Monkey, Viper, Mantis, and Crane followed her.

"Wait!" Po charged after them.

Tigress whirled around to face Po. A hush fell over the room.

"You're staying here!" Her yellow eyes flared.

Anyone else would have crumbled to dust

in the face of an angry Tigress. But Po wasn't going to give in.

"I'm going and you can't stop me!" He tried to walk past Tigress, but she grabbed him by the arm, twisted him around, and tossed him back to the two masters.

"Whoa! Okay, I wasn't ready that time," Po said, dusting himself off.

"Guys, don't," Viper said.

The Five backed away as Tigress went into Hard Style mode.

"Ready!" she cried.

Po pointed at the balcony. "Look!"

Tigress turned, and Po tried to slip past her. Tigress responded with a powerful side kick. Po fell to the ground, but popped up and charged again. Tigress tossed him hard against the wall.

"Stay down!" Viper urged him.

"I have to get to him," Po said, struggling to get back on his feet.

"Then tell me why!" Tigress demanded.

"He was there, okay?" Po blurted out.

"The peacock was there the last time I saw my parents. He knows where I come from, who I am. Look, I'm going. I have to know. The hard core can't understand."

Po walked past Tigress. She leaped at him.

"Tigress, no!" Viper yelled.

But Tigress tackled Po with a hug. Her friends gasped. A hug? From tough Tigress?

"The hard core do understand," she said. "But I can't watch my friend be killed. We're going."

The Furious Five started toward the door once more. Crane glanced at Tigress.

"Hey, maybe you can't watch *me* be killed?"

"Stop being a wimp," Tigress told him.

Monkey smiled. "And . . . she's back."

Po watched helplessly as his friends left without him.

"Don't worry, kid. You're better off here," said Master Ox.

But Po wasn't listening. He wasn't about

to flee like some coward.

He let Shen get away. He couldn't control his visions.

But no matter what happened, he was still the Dragon Warrior—and he was determined to defeat that peacock.

CHAPTER 16

"Stop This Now, Shen"

Gorilla guards safely delivered Soothsayer from the crumbling palace to Shen's command center at the fireworks factory. The peacock proudly puffed up his chest when he saw her.

"What shall we do with her?" a gorilla guard asked.

"It doesn't matter," Shen replied. "Soon my ships will sail from Gongmen City. Once we reach the ocean, all of China will fall before me."

Shen pulled a poker from a cauldron of red-hot coals. An eye symbol glowed hotly from the poker's tip. He moved to the map of China on the wall and burned the eye into Gongmen City.

"Then will you finally be satisfied?" the old goat asked. "Will the subjugation of the whole world finally make you feel better?"

"Well, it's a good start," Shen replied. "I might also convert the basement into a dungeon."

Soothsayer shook her shaggy head. "The cup you choose to fill has no bottom. Stop this now, Shen."

Shen sneered. "Why on earth would I do that?"

"So your parents can rest in peace."

A shadow crossed the peacock's face. "They hated me. Do you understand? They wronged me. And I will make it right."

"They loved you," Soothsayer told him. "They loved you so much that having to send you away killed them."

Shen turned away from Soothsayer. He didn't want her to see the deep sadness inside him. He didn't speak for a while.

When he turned to face her again, his face was a mask of steel.

"The dead exist in the past," he said. "And I must attend to the future." He waved at a gorilla guard.

"Set Soothsayer free. She is no use to me."

"Good-bye, Shen," Soothsayer said. "I wish you happiness."

"Happiness must be taken. And I will take mine," he replied darkly.

Shen didn't watch as Soothsayer was led away. He turned back to the map of China. Soon it would all be his. But he had much work to do.

While Shen was busy making his plans, the Furious Five made their way to the fireworks factory. Without Po, it was easier to move in the darkness without being seen. They hid behind some gun powder kegs where they could see through the factory's open door. Rows and rows of cannons were lined up inside, ready to be moved out.

"If those cannons leave the building, all of China will fall," Tigress said.

"We bring down the building!" Viper suggested.

"Hey, guys!" Mantis called out. "How about this?"

Mantis rubbed some gunpowder between his two front legs. *Poof!* It exploded in his face.

"I'm okay," he said with a grin.

Tigress smiled back. Mantis was on to something.

While the Furious Five made their plan, Po approached the rear of the factory. Nothing could have made him stay behind with Master Ox and Master Croc.

Po pressed himself up against the building's rear wall. Above him, wolf guards paced back and forth on a platform held up by scaffolding made of bamboo poles. Po grabbed a loose pole and swung up to the platform, right behind two wolves.

Thunk! Thunk!

Po quickly knocked out the two guards. Then he held the sleeping bodies in front of him, moving them like puppets. Now he just had to get past the wolf leader. The wolf was muttering to himself. He didn't look happy. And he didn't notice when a disguised Po slipped right past him and entered the factory.

Then Po quickly tossed aside the wolves. A gorilla guard approached, and Po quickly hid behind a crate.

The gorilla nudged the unconscious wolves with his foot. "Hey! On your feet! And wipe those stupid grins off your faces!"

Po carefully made his way through a maze of catwalks above the factory floor. A cloud of steam billowed ahead, and Po saw a familiar shadow inside. He moved to meet it.

Shen stepped through the mist and grinned.

"Greetings, panda."

CHAPTER 17

"Are You Willing to Die to Find the Truth?"

Shen unfurled his tail feathers, revealing the red eye markings. Po gasped and shielded his eyes.

"Tell me what happened that night!" he called out.

"What night?" the peacock asked.

"*That* night," Po yelled back.

"Ah, that night," Shen said.

"Yes!" Po said. "We're talking about the same night, right?"

"Yes, I was there," Shen said coolly. "Yes, I watched as your parents abandoned you. It's a terrible thing. I believe it went something like this!"

Shen pulled a lever, and a bucket suspended from a string swung out, shattering the catwalk under Po's feet. He clutched the bucket to keep from falling as it swung back and forth. He glanced down to see a huge pot of molten metal bubbling underneath him.

While Po hung on for his life, the Furious Five carried out their plan to defeat Shen and destroy the cannon. They pushed a big cart filled with gunpowder kegs through the factory entrance. Monkey smashed a glowing lantern over it. Then Tigress gave one final push.

"Here's your new year's gift!" Monkey called out as wolves scrambled to get away from the cart.

"Hope you like it, cause you can't return it!" Mantis quipped.

Suddenly Tigress spotted Po swinging from a bucket overhead.

"Po?"

Monkey saw him, too. "Return it! Return it!"

The Five frantically worked to put out the flames before the cart exploded. The wolf guards quickly surrounded them. They attacked, burying the Five in a pile of black fur.

Above, Po did his best to hang on.

"Are you willing to die to find out the truth?" Shen asked.

"You bet I am," Po replied. "Though I'd prefer not to."

Po charged at Shen. The peacock unfurled his tail again and spun away, kicking Po as he fled. Po tumbled forward and landed on a conveyor belt loaded with scrap metal. The belt was headed directly for the bubbling pot of molten metal.

Down below, Tigress, Monkey, Viper, Mantis, and Crane expertly tossed the wolves aside. But they were outnumbered.

"We got them!" Mantis told Tigress. "Go!"

With a nod, Tigress bounded off to save Po. He was struggling to keep his balance on the conveyer belt. One wrong move and he'd tumble into the hot metal. But Po grabbed a fork and stabbed it into the belt. Then he jumped off of the side of the belt, still holding onto the fork.

The move saved him. He passed over the bubbling cauldron without falling in. The heat singed the fur on his behind, so he grabbed a frying pan to shield himself.

Shen glared down into the pot, but didn't see Po.

"Looking for me?" Po called out.

Shen turned, but didn't see anything. The conveyor belt traveled back up toward the catwalk. Po rode on the bottom of the belt, armed with the fork and the pan.

"Um . . . I said that too soon, didn't I? *Heeya!*"

Po leaped up to attack Shen. The peacock flashed his tail feathers once more.

"*Waaa!*" Po screamed. Shen raced up to a higher catwalk just as more wolf guards stepped in to attack Po.

"Po!" Tigress yelled.

A wolf leaped at Tigress, and she grabbed him in midair. Then she flung the wolf at the wolves attacking Po.

Crash! The wolves tumbled off the catwalk, freeing Po. He hopped to his feet and climbed after Shen.

"No! Wait!" Tigress cried.

But there was no stopping Po. He wanted answers, and he was going to get them. He caught up to the peacock, cornering him against a big box covered by a cloth.

"No more running, Shen!" Po shouted.

"So it seems," the peacock agreed.

"Now! Answers!" Po demanded angrily.

"You want to know so badly?" Shen asked. "You think knowing will heal you, huh? Fill some crater in your soul? Well, here's your answer: Your parents didn't love you. But here, let me heal you."

He yanked the cloth off of the huge box behind him. But it wasn't a box—it was a huge cannon. Po's eyes widened in fear.

Before he could run, Shen scraped his claws over the cannon, creating a spark. He lit the fuse.

Kaboom!

Po flew across the factory, over the heads of the Furious Five and into the night sky beyond.

"Noooo!" Tigress cried.

CHAPTER 18

"Who Are You, Panda?"

Over in the Dragon Grotto, Master Shifu was peacefully meditating. Then his eyes popped open. Thunder boomed in the distance, and jagged lightning streaked the sky.

Something terrible had happened.

Far away, outside Gongmen City, Po's unconscious body floated down the river. He came to a low, half-moon bridge, but his belly was too big to pass underneath it. His body bobbed in the water until someone came and poked it gently with a walking stick.

It was nighttime when Po finally woke to the sensation of cold raindrops splattering on his face. He could feel acupuncture needles on his arms and legs. He slowly opened his eyes to find himself in an old, run-down hut. Rain poured through holes in the old straw roof. Across the room, the old goat was making a pot of tea over a small stove.

Slowly, Po sat up. His whole body ached, but he had to get away. He tried to crawl across the floor, but the goat peeked behind her. He closed his eyes, playing dead. All was silent. When he opened his eyes again, Soothsayer was right next to him.

"*Ahh!*" Po jumped in fright, then winced in pain. He was really hurting.

Soothsayer held out a steaming cup of liquid. Po was still suspicious.

"Yeah, like you could make me drink tha—"

The goat swiftly stuck a long, thin acupuncture needle into Po's forehead, causing his mouth to open automatically. She dumped the contents of the cup in his mouth and took out the needle. Po closed his mouth and swallowed.

"Blech!" Po complained, coughing.

"If I wanted you dead, I would have left you in that river," Soothsayer told him.

"Why save me?" Po asked.

"So you can fulfill your destiny," she replied.

"What are you talking about?" Po raised his arms in the air. "Where am I? What is this place?"

"I'm surprised you remember so little," Soothsayer said. "But you were so little when it happened . . ."

A quick vision flashed across his mind . . . flames . . . screams . . .

"Yaaa!" Po yelled. Shaken, he crawled to the edge of the hut.

"Perhaps you do remember," Soothsayer said.

"What? It's just a stupid nightmare," Po said.

"Nightmare? Or memory?" Soothsayer asked.

Po gazed out of the window and looked

at the river running near the hut. He could see his own reflection in the water. Old memories were bubbling up now. His reflection transformed into the face of baby Po. The vision unfolded before him now, like he was in the audience watching a play. It wasn't raining in his memory . . .

The sun was shining brightly on a thriving panda village. Adult pandas harvested radishes in a lush, green field. Young pandas chased one another laughing. Po's mother and father watched red box kites flying in the blue sky overhead. And tiny baby Po crawled out of his family's hut, clutching a stuffed panda doll.

"This was a thriving village," Soothsayer narrated as Po watched the vision, spellbound. "Young Shen was in line to rule Gongmen City. I foretold that someone would stand in his way. A panda. But I never could have foretold what came next."

The happy scene changed in front of Po's eyes . . .

It was night and Shen and his wolf guards

ransacked the burning panda village. A frightened baby Po sat in front of the hut, clutching his doll. Then Shen appeared in front of him, flanked by two guards. The wolves leaped at baby Po . . .

Po's father bravely ran in front of Po, holding the only weapon he had: a rake. He struck the two wolves and they tumbled backward, knocking into Shen. The peacock fell into the fire, singeing his claws.

Po's mother quickly picked up baby Po and fled into the forest. The tiny panda lost his grip on his doll. It landed in the dirt under the hut and then was buried under falling debris.

Now, years later, Po spotted the discarded doll on the ground in front of the hut. He picked it up. He remembered it all now. Po gently dropped the doll and reached out to catch a falling raindrop, moving his arms as Master Shifu had taught him.

"Stop fighting," Soothsayer told him. "Let it flow."

The red eye flashed as Po's mother raced through the trees. Then the wolves came with their

snapping jaws.

Po moved the drop from hand to hand. It didn't break.

Breathless, Po's mother reached the edge of the forest. There she found a radish cart. She stashed baby Po in one of the baskets. The wolves were getting closer and closer.

With tears in her eyes, she reached down to kiss her baby one last time. Then she left him, drawing the wolves and Shen away from the radish basket.

Po's hand swung down, and the unbroken drop gently splashed on a tiny flower poking out of the dirt.

"Your story may not have such a happy beginning, but that doesn't make you who you are," Soothsayer said softly. "It is the rest of your story. Who you choose to be. So who are you, panda?"

Po slowly stood up. His eyes shone with determination.

"I am Po. And I'm gonna need a hat."

CHAPTER 19

"A Panda Stands Between You
and Your Destiny!"

Shen's armada of boats floated in the canals flowing through Gongmen City. Shen was perched on a royal platform on the largest boat, surrounded by two large cannons. The Furious Five were chained together, prisoners of Shen.

"Such sad, sad faces," he remarked as he strolled past them. "But now is a time only for joy. You are going to be part of something beautiful."

He stood face-to-face with Tigress. She growled menacingly.

"Once we reach the harbor, in front of all

the world, you and your precious kung fu will die," Shen told her. "Then China will know to bow before me."

He waved his wing and the chain holding the warriors was yanked up, suspending them in the air above the boat. Shen grinned and then returned to his platform to watch the destruction.

"Honestly, even though I'm a kung fu warrior, I always figured my death would be a result of . . . I've told you guys about my dad, right?" asked Mantis.

"Yes," answered Viper and Crane, rolling their eyes.

"We cannot give up hope," Monkey said. "Po would want us to remain strong. Hard core. Right, Tigress?"

But Tigress didn't answer. A tear rolled down her cheek.

The fleet of boats approached a bridge blocking them from reaching the river.

"Nothing stands in my way!" Shen bellowed.

Boom! Boom! Shen's gunners targeted the bridge. Innocent pigs and bunnies scurried across the bridge, fearful of the cannons.

"You coward!" Tigress screamed at Shen.

While everyone was running away from the cannons, in the distance, a tiny speck was running *toward* the cannons. Tigress noticed it first. Her eyes widened.

"Po," she realized.

Po stopped running and perched defiantly on a rooftop. He wore a wide-brimmed, round straw hat and his cape was flapping in the wind. The Dragon Warrior!

Monkey, Viper, Crane, and Mantis saw him, too. "Po?"

Shen was furious. "How many times do I have to kill the same stinking panda!"

Po's gaze was focused on Shen. Then he caught sight of the size of Shen's army. He paused. They were outnumbered. How would they . . . Then Po noticed his friends. Seeing the Furious Five tied up and surrounded by Shen's army made Po furious. He narrowed

119

his gaze at the peacock again.

Po shouted heroically across the battlefield. "A panda stands between you and your destiny!"

Po was still far away, and Shen could barely hear him.

"What?" Shen called back.

Po called out another threat. "Prepare yourself for a hot serving of justice! And now, free the Five! The Disc of Destruction!"

He took off his hat and flung it. It went about three feet and fluttered into the canal, hitting some wolf soldiers.

"Oops," Po said sheepishly.

"Take aim!" Shen shouted.

The soldiers trained every cannon barrel on Po. He jumped off of the roof, away from the aim of the cannons.

"Get him! Just get him!" Shen fumed.

The gunners struggled to re-aim the heavy cannons. Po zigzagged across the battlefield, moving closer and closer as the gunners tried to get a lock on him. They aimed the cannons left, then right. Left, then right.

Then Po dove right in the middle of the wolf soldiers on the battlefield! Now the gunner's cannons were not only trained on Po, but at all of the foot soldiers, too.

"Don't shoot! Don't shoot!" a wolf gunner shouted frantically.

"*You* don't shoot!" shouted the gunner opposite him.

"I won't shoot if you won't shoot!" the first gunner called back.

The gunners had to hold off. Po fought his way through the army, delivering kung fu chops and powerful kicks. The cannons couldn't lock aim on him.

"Don't shoot! Don't shoot!" cried the wolf leader.

"Someone better shoot!" Shen yelled. "Attack!"

Every wolf on the field descended on Po. He used his strong belly to blast a group off of him, sending them flying. Then he jumped to his feet and attacked them once more.

At the same time, the Furious Five were trying to free themselves. Po grabbed a battle-ax from one of the wolves and tossed it toward his friends.

"Catch of Freedom!" Po yelled.

Monkey snagged the ax with his tail and cut the chain holding the Five. They quickly raced to the battlefield to join Po.

"Impressive, Dragon Warrior," Tigress told him. "What's your plan?"

"Step one, free the Five!" Po replied.

"What's step two?" Viper asked.

"Uh . . . honestly, I didn't even think I'd get *this* far," Po admitted. "Uh, stop Shen before he gets to the harbor!"

They plowed through the wolf and gorilla soldiers, making their way back to Shen. Monkey wrapped his tail around a wolf's neck and spun around him while kicking out and sending wolves flying. Charging wolves collided with Po's generous belly and fell backward, unconscious. Crane used his long beak like a fighting stick. Viper used her lightning moves to wrap her body around a gorilla's arm and then slammed him hard into the ground. Tigress knocked down soldier after soldier with her powerful punches and kicks. And Mantis used his small size to deliver stunning surprise attacks with his strong legs. The soldiers never saw him coming.

Po conked a wolf on the head and tossed him in the air.

"Viper! Puppet of Death!" he cried.

Viper wrapped her coils around the wolf, working him like a puppet.

"Tigress!" she called out.

Tigress bounded up and Viper jumped on her back with the wolf puppet. She forced his arms to move, taking out other wolf soldiers with his swords.

Suddenly Master Ox and Master Croc appeared, tossing wolves aside as they came to aid the Furious Five and the Dragon Warrior.

"Your friend here is very persuasive," Master Ox answered, nodding behind him.

Master Shifu soared through the air, twirling his battle staff.

"Master Shifu!" Po shouted in surprise.

"Quickly! Use their boats to block the way!" Shifu yelled.

Tigress jumped onto a boat and kicked a cannon. The boat tipped right over. Po planted one foot on one boat and one foot on another and then grabbed the sails so he could ride them at the same time. Crane swooped in.

"I got your back, Po!" he cried.

Crane flapped his wings, and the air inflated the sails. Po steered toward the growing pile of wrecked boats.

"Woo hoo! Sail of Justice!" Po cheered.

The plan was working. The canal was blocked. Shen would never get through with his cannons now. He watched from his perch, growing angrier and angrier each moment.

Now the kung fu warriors had to get to Shen to stop him for good. They fought side by side, flipping gorilla guards and wolf soldiers like pancakes.

"I love you guys," Po told his friends.

Shen anxiously paced back and forth. "Why aren't we firing?" he asked the wolf leader.

"They're taking out our gunners, sir," the leader replied. "They're getting close!"

"Fire! Fire!" Shen cried, panicked. "Fire at them!"

"But sir, we'll kill our own," the wolf protested.

Shen's red eyes blazed with fury. "I said fire at them! Fire!"

But the wolf leader wouldn't do it. "No!"

Two thin blades shot out from under Shen's sleeves, knocking the wolf leader into the water. Shen leaped onto the cannon and turned it on the kung fu warriors. Then he scraped his claw along the metal. A spark shot up . . .

Kaboom! Kaboom! Kaboom!

Cannonballs tore through the battlefield. The explosions sent Shen's soldiers flying. The Furious Five sailed through the air and crashed into the river. Master Shifu, Master Ox, and Master Croc were knocked off of their feet. Po landed on a piece of wood floating in the water.

Po raised his head with a groan. His friends were hurt—badly. Shen's cannons had done exactly what he said they would. They had beaten kung fu.

CHAPTER 20

"Battle's Over, Shen!"

Tigress floated past Po, her eyes closed. He pulled her to him.

"Tigress?"

She couldn't answer him. Po slowly started to paddle his piece of wood down the river, taking Tigress with him. Shen grinned smugly, savoring his victory.

Po reached an overturned boat jutting out of the water. He stood up on it and suddenly stopped and turned around. He faced the cannons, his eyes closed in concentration. Shen's smile faded.

"As you wish." He turned to his gunners. "Let's finish him!"

Po's friends tried to get up to help him, but they weren't able to recover from the cannon blasts. They watched helplessly as the gunners trained a large cannon directly on Po.

"Fire!" Shen yelled.

BOOM! A cannonball sizzled through the air. Po opened his eyes to see the ball coming toward him and then closed his eyes again. In his mind, he pictured the cannonball as a large drop of water.

Inner Peace, he told himself.

Without looking, he reached out with one paw. The cannonball bounced off and careened into the mountains behind him, exploding as it hit the rocks.

The whole battlefield went silent. Nobody could believe what they had just seen. Po opened his eyes and saw that his hand was on fire.

"Yeooow!" he cried, shaking his hand until the fire died out. Then he settled into a kung fu pose, waiting for the next attack.

"Again!" Shen cried.

Boom! Boom! Boom! Po gracefully deflected each cannonball as it reached him, redirecting them to destroy Shen's own ships.

Shen was overcome with fury. "Kill him! Somebody kill him!" he shrieked.

"Yes, Lord Shen," a gorilla gunner replied.

Boom! Boom! Boom! Boom! Cannonballs filled the sky.

Boom! Boom! Boom! Boom! The cannonballs hit Shen's cannons, shattering them into pieces. Shen watched in horror as his beautiful weapons were destroyed before his eyes.

"Wait, no!" he cried, panicked. "Cease fire! Cease fire!"

But another cannonball was already on its way to Po. He hit it back, this time aiming it right at Shen.

Kaboom!

A cloud of black smoke covered the water. When it cleared, Shen was underneath the shadow of a destroyed cannon. He gave a cough, looking around at the destroyed boats and cannons that littered the water. Po appeared next to him.

"How did you do it?" Shen asked in disbelief.

Po shrugged. "You know, you just keep your elbows up, and keep the shoulders loose—"

"Not the cannons," Shen said. "How did you get over it? You lost your parents, everything. It must have scarred you for life."

"See, that's the thing, Shen," Po said. "Scars heal."

"No, they don't," Shen pointed out. "*Wounds* heal."

He was right. "Oh yeah," Po said. "What do scars do? They fade, I guess?"

"I don't care what scars do!" Shen said angrily.

"You should, Shen," Po said. "You gotta let go of that stuff from the past 'cause it just doesn't matter. The only thing that matters . . . is what you choose to be now."

Shen looked thoughtful. "You're right," he

130

said, after a moment. The blades popped out from his sleeves. "Then I choose this!"

Shen lunged forward to attack, but Po easily dodged the lethal blades. He knocked Shen backward, and the blades shattered.

"Battle's over," Po told him. "You don't have to keep acting all evil!"

Shen unfurled his tail feathers, revealing blades tucked between them.

Po was impressed. "Whoa."

Shen spun around, swinging the blades on his tail. Po jumped back and grabbed a wooden board just as the blades came flying toward him. They thudded safely into the board.

Shen grabbed a sword and advanced on Po. He swung and accidentally sliced through the wooden supports holding the heavy cannon.

The cannon rolled and landed on top of some barrels. They were full of black powder! There was a spark and then—

Boom!

Po was tossed into the water.

In the sky, brilliant fireworks popped and sparkled over Gongmen City.

"Oooh!" The citizens cheered at the sight.

Po swam up to the surface and felt a strong paw grab his hand. It was Tigress. She pulled him onto the shore and he looked into her eyes gratefully.

Master Ox, Master Croc, Master Shifu, and the rest of the Furious Five raced to greet Po.

Master Shifu looked up at him. "It seems you have found Inner Peace. And at such a young age." He bowed to his student.

"Well, I had a pretty good teacher," Po said with a smile.

CHAPTER 21

"I Love You, Dad!"

Balance. It's something every kung fu master must learn.

Tigress had a hard core and a soft heart. Balanced.

Po was the Dragon Warrior, but he also helped make soup in a noodle shop. He lost his real parents long ago, but he also had a father who loved him very much.

That father, Mr. Ping, was trying to placate a mother pig and her son.

"What do you mean he's not here?" the mother complained. "It's my son's birthday. All he wanted was to meet the Dragon Warrior."

"How about some tofu birthday cake instead, eh?" Mr. Ping suggested.

The mother pig stood up. "You know, I think we'll just try again some other time. When do you think he'll be back?"

The question broke Mr. Ping's heart. "I don't know, okay!" he blurted out. "Maybe never!"

He sat down and buried his head in his wings.

"Why did he have to go save China?" he sobbed. "I mean, I know why, but *why*?"

Suddenly, the little boy pig began to laugh excitedly. Mr. Pig turned to see what the fuss was about. He saw Po standing in the doorway of the noodle shop!

"Po? Is that you?" Mr. Ping asked.

For an instant, Mr. Ping saw cute little baby Po, sitting in his radish basket. Now grown-up Po was standing before him. He was really back!

"Ahhhh," Mr. Ping cried happily. He rushed over to Po. "So how did it go, son? Did you find what you were looking for?"

"Yep," Po replied.

"I knew you would!" Mr. Ping exclaimed. "That's why I had new signs made. 'My son saved China; you, too, can save—buy one dumpling, get one free.'"

"That's a pretty good deal," Po said.

"Would you like to try one?"

"Um, maybe later," Po replied. "There's something I should tell you."

Mr. Ping looked nervous. Had he lost Po forever?

"While I was gone, I found out where I was born, who my parents were, and where I came from," Po said. "I know who I am."

"You do?" Mr. Ping asked.

"I'm your son," Po told him. He pulled his dad into a big hug. "I love you, Dad."

"I love you, too, son," his father said tearfully.

Peeking behind Po, Mr. Ping saw two full baskets of radishes. It was time to make some soup!

"Ahh! Delicious, fat radishes!" Mr. Ping exclaimed. He picked up one of the baskets and brought it into the kitchen.

Po picked up the other basket.

"You're probably hungry, though," Mr. Ping said. "Let me make you something to eat."

"What are you talking about?" Po asked. "I'll cook."

"No, I'll cook," insisted Mr. Ping.

"Dad—"

"It's the least I can do," said his father. "You saved China."

"It's the least *I* can do," Po countered. "You raised me."

"Po—"

"Dad—"

"Po—"

"Okay, how about this?" Po asked. "We both cook. Together."

Mr. Ping thought about this.

"No, I'll cook!"

Po had found his balance once more.

And because of Po, balance was returning to China, too.

Far, far away from the Valley of Peace, in a valley hidden in the mountains, a monk meditated inside a temple. The monk, a panda, saw a vision that brought him great joy.

"My son is alive!" he said.

He lowered his hood and rushed out onto the temple steps. Below him, hundreds of villagers turned their heads expectantly.

Every single one of them was a panda.